STORYLINES - TELLING MOVIES IN WORDS

ZUBIE SAURABH SENGUPTA

Contents

Preface

It has been one of my most cherished dreams to have a book published. However, having always been involved in the audio-visual medium as a writer-director in advertising, television and now feature films, stories in my mind do not take shape in the form of a novel or short stories. Instead, they invariably develop in the form of storylines for movies. In this book, I am presenting you some such storylines for your reading pleasure.

Acknowledgements

Dr.Sushma Sengupta
Sidharth Sengupta
Sujata Sengupta
Shona Chatterjee
Shadab Khan
Mohan Menon
Gazala Shaikh
Smitha Seshadri
Prabha Sinha
Rajat Dhar
Dr.Raj Bhramhbhatt

EDITOR
Naresh Kumar

About The Author

Son of Maj. Gen. (Dr.) Sukumar Sengupta and Dr. Sushma Sengupta. Zubie Saurabh Sengupta, as a writer-director, started his career in advertising and then expanded his horizon to television and now, as a writer-director, he has made his foray into movies with Hindi Feature Film, 'IN THE MONTH OF JULY', now streaming on several known OTTs and 'IT'S A MAN'S WORLD' He also has to his credit, as a singer, composer, lyricist, poet and narrator, a bouquet of audio albums released on reputed digital platforms worldwide.

CHAPTER ONE

REAL MAN

A man chooses to live as a eunuch for the sake of his loved ones.

When floods strike Lacchagir – a small village in the interiors of Uttar Pradesh by the banks of river Ganga – within hours the entire village gets immersed in water. Many lives are lost and many more rendered homeless. Even hopes of revival are lost when the compensation granted by the Government is swallowed by corrupt officials and never reaches the victims.

Amongst these victims is twenty-seven-year-old Hariya, who used to earn his modest living as a farmer. The natural calamity has snatched away his only means of survival and most of his family members, leaving behind only his wife Manju, his four-year-old son Shiv and his five-month-old son Panku, whom he manages to save through great effort.

But despite such hopeless circumstances, Hariya firmly holds on to his dream of creating a beautiful life for his loved ones and of building a great future for his sons. "I will make my sons into big men," he always asserts staunchly.

With this dream in his heart, Hariya, along with his wife and children arrives in Mumbai – the city of dreams. For Hariya, the only lead to this big city is his friend Gokul, who works at a factory and lives in a *basti* with his parents, trying to make ends meet.

Gokul helps Hariya find a *kholi* in the basti and even pays the deposit for it with the understanding that Hariya would take care of the rent and return the deposit once he starts earning money. To help Hariya find a job, Gokul takes him to many places, but they are always met with disappointment, for either the person in-charge asks for bribes or he favours his own people over Hariya. Some even ask Hariya to work free for six months till he learns the job.

Given the urgency to start making money so he could return Gokul's loan and take care of his own family, Hariya starts working as a labourer at a construction site on daily wages. But here too, the wages are too little. Also, the Asst. Manager authorized to pay out the wages grabs his own cut from the remuneration. Scared of losing their jobs, Hariya and the other laborers keep silent.

Survival, thus, becomes tough for Hariya. Burdened to provide for his family, pay the kholi's rent and haunted by his dream of building his son's future, Hariya finds himself struggling greatly.

In this daily struggle, Hariya is often offered tea by his co-worker Bhushan at the small tea-shop next to a traffic signal near the construction site. Here, he witnesses some eunuchs (Hijras) demanding money from people. Initially, Hariya shows pity on them. But then, Bhushan quips, "You don't know how much money they make. They make in two days what you and I will earn in a month. That one – Luxmi – she has two taxis running in Mumbai. And Reshma over there has a pan-shop to her name. It's not only on the streets, they also make money from shops, houses, offices on every occasion – weddings, births, parties, grih-pravesh, festivals, inaugurations and the works. You have no idea how great it is for them to be a Hijra."

That day onwards, Hariya's perspective about eunuchs changes completely. Whenever he feels frustrated by his trying circumstances, he compares himself to the eunuchs who earn so much more than him. This comparison fuels in him an intense hatred towards the eunuchs that borders on jealousy.

Then, in a fateful phase, Panku, his five-month-old child, falls terribly ill. After getting tests done, for which he has to sell off Manju's *mangal-sutra*, the doctors inform him that Panku's blood is defective and he has to undergo complete blood replacement every 15 days for treatment, which would cost a lot of money.

Unable to see his child suffering and unable to bear the pain in Manju's eyes, Hariya finds himself pushed against the wall. Yet to save his ailing child he finds no door to turn to. Even Gokul's financial struggles kept him from being able to help Hariya.

One night, as Hariya flusters over having only a handful of days to resolve this crisis, an idea dawns upon him. "Why can't I act as a eunuch?" he thinks. With Gokul's help, he could find a loan from somewhere and then repay it by earning it as a eunuch.

When with a hardened heart he shares this decision with Manju, she is flabbergasted. But driven by desperation, Hariya convinces her. He tells her that this is the only way for them to fulfil all of their dreams – decent food, shelter, clothing, good education for their children, and in the end, a beautiful tomorrow. Eventually, Manju warms up to the hope of a great future and decide to support Hariya's decision.

She starts dressing up Hariya as a woman and trains him to act feminine. And what had once seemed gory now transforms into a moment of fun between husband and wife.

Every day, Hariya secretly sneaks out of the basti, dressed as a eunuch and starts demanding money at the traffic signals. But he never knew that the ride was not going be a smooth one.

Unofficially, the city is divided in territories between different hijra groups. And no one encroaches upon the other's territory. So, when Hariya starts working at the traffic signal, the other hijras protest vehemently since he was not part of their group. But Hariya does not pay heed to their protests. He arrogantly and aggressively fights all protests and antagonism that come his way and continues to demand money at the signal. The struggle is hard. But by the end of the day, when he sees the money in his hands, he finds his struggles worth the smiles on his family's faces.

But all the happiness that he brings to his family are suddenly shattered when one night, while the whole family is enjoying a special mutton curry that Manju has prepared, some thugs barge into Hariya's kholi, beat him senseless and drag him away with them even as Manju's cries for help fall on deaf ears while the people in the basti stand silently and watch this mayhem.

Manju rushes to Gokul who takes her to file a report at the police station. But the police instead of filing an FIR complaint, harass Manju and Gokul and send them away.

Hariya, meanwhile, is taken to a *chawl* inhabited totally by the hijras, and in a dingy hall, he is beaten up brutally. As he lies on the floor, broken and battered, Tara, the head of the chawl, walks up to him and says, "If you ever try to enter my territory again, not just you, but your entire family will be killed!"

Hariya, in turn, tells her how helpless he is and that this is the only way he can save his sick child. Hearing Hariya's story and after some deliberation, Tara offers him two options, "Either you stay away from my territory OR you JOIN me. I will pay the entire amount for your child's treatment in advance, but you must join my group. Which means you will have to stay in our community, in this chawl, and do exactly what I ask you to do. Take this night to make a decision."

When a shaken up Hariya reaches home that night and tells Manju of the situation, she refuses the idea completely, for she cannot imagine living away from him. But when Hariya insists that this is the only way to save their child, and then promises her that he would regularly come to meet her clandestinely, so no one ever comes to know about it, Manju agrees to Hariya going and living in the Hijra community.

Next day, when Hariya stands before Tara, she orders her henchman to send money to Hariya's wife for their son's treatment. Then, to Hariya, she says, "From today, your name is no longer 'Hariya'. You are now 'Meena'. And to become 'Meena', you will first and foremost develop BREASTS!"

Hariya is shocked by this statement and is left speechless. Tara, meanwhile, continues, "If you do not agree to it, I will take back the money for your son's treatment right away, and never give you this opportunity ever again. The decision is yours."

Hariya bows down his head helplessly. His silence is evidence to his agreement to Tara's demand.

Weak and forlorn, Hariya makes a phone call to the Beedi shop close to the kholi and asks the shop owner to call Manju on phone. When he hears Manju's voice on the phone, he feels desperate to express his agony to her. But he controls himself and does not tell her that he was going for a breast implant surgery. Instead, he tells her that Tara was sending him to Delhi for a function. He promises Manju that he will meet her once he comes back.

After the operation, when Hariya looks at himself in the mirror for the first time, he is devastated and realizes he will always find himself disgusting. A shattered Hariya calls up Gokul, asking him to meet in a secluded place. Later that night, in a dilapidated building, when Hariya comes to meet Gokul, Gokul is stunned to see Hariya's new avatar.

After explaining the entire situation, Hariya tells Gokul that he was too ashamed to face Manju and has hence decided not to visit her at all. He asks Gokul to take care of his family's needs on his behalf, making Gokul the connecting point between Hariya and his family. Hariya frequently meets Gokul to handover his earnings for the family.

Manju keeps waiting for the day Hariya would come to meet her, but all she gets is the money sent by him. She keeps asking Gokul if he received any news of Hariya. Gokul, however, tells her that Hariya was on a country-wide trip and that he had no clue when he'll be back.

Meanwhile, Gokul tries to bring some joy in Manju and the children's lives as much as he can, not realizing that the basti people were watching his visits with a sceptical eye. Rumour-mongers start spreading gossip that Manju was a characterless woman having an affair with Gokul. Her tainted image gives courage to other men in the basti to start making passes at her, the most overbearing of whom is the money lender, Kashinath.

Kashinath never misses a chance of hinting at a sexual encounter, but Manju swallows his misbehaviour silently, never telling Gokul about it. After all, Gokul was putting all his efforts into getting her son Shiv's admission in a good school. Finally, one reputed school agrees to admit Shiv, but on the condition that a sum of one lakh rupees be paid as donation.

Meanwhile, Hariya struggles to cope with living amongst hijras. In the chawl, he has to share a room with a eunuch named Kajal. Initially, Hariya finds himself a misfit in the community. He remains a recluse, confined to his room, not sharing or participating in any of the daily activities of the group, seeing which, Tara ensures that Hariya's food is sent to his room.

Hariya despises interacting with the other hijras. He hates them all. But gradually, seeing their efforts to make him comfortable, brighten his spirit, his hatred starts to melt. He realizes that the eunuchs have been shunned by the society for none of their fault. That they are not given any decent job to help them survive. That they are deprived of the joys of living in a family. And that they are left with no option other than to adopt this obnoxious life.

In time, Hariya grows warm towards them and becomes great friends with them all. Kajal, whom he once hated, eventually becomes his best friend. So much so that he even shares with her that he had been secretly sending money to his family.

When Hariya learns about the demand of rupees one lakh for Shiv's admission, he has no one else but Kajal to share his frustration with. Its then that Kajal reveals that she and some other eunuchs had also been sending good money to their families without Tara's knowledge. She tells him about the prostitution which they were secretly practicing to make some extra money and tells him that the real money was in fact in sex trade.

Hariya is shocked at first at the very thought of prostitution. But then, remembering that his greatest dream is to make his son a big man, Hariya gives in and agrees to step into the game of prostitution. Thus, to give his son a life of pride, he dives into a life of ultimate shame.

The first time he is sodomized by a man, he goes through great physical, mental and emotional trauma. But over time, he becomes numb to the experience and starts practicing prostitution mechanically. Ironically, around the same time, Manju struggles hard to protect her dignity from voyeuristic advances by debauch men in the basti, even as she is waiting longingly for Hariya to come to her one day.

As her patience starts running out and her spirit starts to fail, Gokul tries his best to cheer her and boost her children's morale. One such day, seeing Manju terribly depressed, Gokul persuades her to accompany him to the function of his co-worker's son's naming ceremony.

At the function, while all others are celebrating, Manju sits gloomily in a corner, recalling how Hariya and she had rejoiced over Shiv's birth. Just then, a group of hijras barge into the function and start dancing. And Manju is left shocked, for among the eunuchs, she sees Hariya too, dancing among them!

As Hariya's *pallu* falls, exposing his buxom body, his eyes meet Manju's. His head then hangs in shame. Unable to face Manju, he walks out. But Manju promptly follows him and stops him on the road. "So this is why you stayed away from me," she cries. "Do you think I love you only for your body? Is that all our relationship is about?"

Manju hugs Hariya and cries profusely. Just then, Hariya notices other people from the function coming out. He parts away from Manju saying people might see them. Manju says she will only stop following him if he promises to meet her. Hariya gives in. He tells her that he will come to the kholi in the night. As Manju leaves, Hariya says, "Manju make sure our children are not there in the kholi when I come. I don't want them to see me like this." That night, Manju sends her children to Gokul's house.

Later that night, after everyone in the chawl has gone to sleep, Hariya tries to sneak out. But just as he reaches the exit door, he finds Kajal standing in front of him. "With what face will you meet your family?" she asks. "You have a body of a half-woman. You have been sodomized by men day and night. And yet you call yourself a man? Can you ever be a proper husband? A proper father? No! You are as good as a *namard*!"

Hariya swallows Kajal's words and leaves. Yet the entire way to Manju, Kajal's words hammer his mind.

Cloaked in a blanket, Hariya slips into the basti and makes it to his kholi, where he finds Manju all dressed for him. She ushers him in and closes the door and hugs him firmly. But Hariya is uncomfortable. He shrugs her aside. Looking away from her, he confesses, "I am not good for you anymore, Manju. I am tainted. My body is spoilt. Not only do I not have a body of a proper man, I have also been used sexually by other men. I just came to tell you that you must forget me now. That you must think I have become a namard."

Manju watches how broken, how shattered, Hariya is. She sees how his self-esteem has hit rock bottom. But she walks up to him, sits in front of him and gently plants a kiss on his lips. Slowly, she takes off his and her own clothes and takes him into firm embrace. That night, Hariya and Manju make love with great passion. And finally, fall asleep in each other's arms.

Hours later, while they are in deep sleep, a heavy knock rattles their door. Hariya quickly hides himself in the small kitchen, while Manju opens the door. A dead drunk Kashinath is standing at the door, forcing Manju to come with him. Hariya can see Kashinath imposing himself on Manju, but he cannot do anything about it.

After much resistance from Manju, when Kashinath grabs her hand and starts dragging her out of the kholi, Hariya is unable to contain his anger. Outraged, like a volcano, he erupts and pounces on Kashinath and starts beating him like a maniac. Kashinath cries for help and some basti people gather to stop the commotion. But driven by frenzy, Hariya cannot stop beating Kashinath.

Finally, police arrive at the scene and take Hariya away. Panic-stricken Manju rushes to Gokul's house for help.

Inside the police-lock-up, Hariya is tortured and abused. Finally, he is left on his own when he becomes a lifeless object. Gokul arrives soon after and gets Hariya released.

As they are traveling back to Gokul's house, Hariya is lost in thoughts. After a long silence, he says, "Gokul, you always wanted to start your own shop. I can arrange the money for it. But in return you will have to do me a favour. Will you?"

Gokul looks at him questioningly.

Lost in contemplation, when Hariya enters Gokul's house, Manju tells him that the children had gone to sleep so he need not worry. As Manju gets him water, he says, "Manju, I always wanted a beautiful life for you. And a great future for Shiv and Panku. This has been my only dream, my only wish in life. Do you want my wish to get fulfilled?"

"Why are you asking this?" Manju asks.

Hariya says, "Because today you can fulfil my wish."

Manju is perplexed.

"Will you fulfil my wish?" Hariya asks again.

"I will do anything to fulfil your every wish," Manju answers.

With a firm face, Hariya then says, "Get married to Gokul."

Manju is stunned. She has no words to say.

Hariya goes on, "Try to understand Manju. If you marry Gokul, he will protect you from all the vultures of the world. You will be able to move in the society with a decent husband. Our children will have a father whom they can respect. With me, you will only face shame. If not for your sake and not for our children's sake, hold Gokul's hand for my sake. Nothing will make me happier than seeing you,

Shiv and Panku have a happy home with Gokul. Tell me. Will you fulfil my wish?"

Manju breaks down, and tears filled in her eyes, she slaps Hariya frenziedly before she finally drops to the floor crying.

As wedding rituals go on in full gusto, Gokul and Manju sit nervously. Manju is holding a storm of pain inside her and Gokul is hiding his tension. After the wedding, in a grand celebration, a group of eunuchs arrive and break into a vigorous dance. The one leading this group is none other than Hariya, who is dancing with mad joy.

Manju's eyes are full with tears as she watches Hariya dancing. Later, as Gokul and Manju leave in a Maruti van with the children while Hariya watches them leave.

Later that night, as Hariya sits by the entrance of the chawl, reminiscing all the beautiful moments he had spent with Manju and their children, Tara comes and sits next to him. For the first time, she appears concerned for him. She says, "So at last you have fulfilled all your responsibilities. Aren't you happy?"

"I am happy," Hariya replies chokingly. "My wife found a real man to call a 'Husband'. And my kids found a real man to call a 'Father' "

Tara tenderly replies, "No, Hariya. He's not a real man. *You* are a real man."

Unable to contain his anguish anymore, Hariya breaks down. Tara holds him to console him. That whole night, Hariya cries profusely resting his head on Tara's lap.

THE END

CHAPTER TWO

EVERYTHING BUT LOVE

Trapped in the closet, a forlorn homosexual man longs
for true love.

Shabby, unkempt and worn out, twenty-eight-year-old Rohit Sarkar clearly reflects a man who does not love himself. Holding on to an intense dream of becoming a successful novelist, Rohit's struggle to fulfil his dream is leading him nowhere. To add to his misery, on the personal front, Rohit's journey has been infested with a never-ending series of heart-breaks, for being a closeted homosexual, he could never express the strong feelings he developed for the men he came across down his path.

A lonely suffering, which he could not share with anyone overpowers him with frustration and gloom. Until one day, his elder cousin, Mohan, suggests him to meet a clairvoyant with a proven track record who could guide Rohit in the right direction.

Hence, Rohit goes for a private session with renowned clairvoyant Tushar Shain. Her presence is so soothing and serene that Rohit pours out his anguish to her uninhibitedly. He honestly expresses his feelings, "I have two goals in life. First, I want to become a successful author. And second, I want a life-partner."

Tushar studies him keenly and replies, "Only one thing can change your destiny."

"What?" Rohit curiously asks.

"A woman," Tushar replies. "If you want to get out of this stuck situation, bring a woman into your life. Get married."

Rohit is flustered. "How can that be? I am searching for a male life-partner."

"You cannot achieve both the goals," Tushar emphasizes. "You will have to forego one for another. You have two options in front of you. Get married to have a life full of name, fame, wealth and social standing, while always wanting true love. Or live a life with no name, no fame, no wealth, no social standing. Live a simple, ordinary existence, but one with lots of love."

Tushar's words have a strong impact on Rohit. And after much deliberation, he opts for a life full of name and fame and wealth and social standing. This is how Meghna enters his life as his bride. Traditional, graceful and beautiful, Meghna is the ideal woman every man would like to marry.

Yet for Rohit, she is just a means to escalate his prospects of becoming a celebrated author. And not much after marriage, Rohit's career-graph starts soaring. He achieves great heights of success. Yet on the personal level, his heart remains empty. No matter how much loving and caring Meghna is, Rohit is never able to feel true love for her.

Even as Rohit remains aloof, Meghna makes all the efforts to evoke love in him. All Rohit can manage in return is to pretend to be in love with her. Deep inside, he knows that his display of love and affection towards her is only superficial, and not something coming from his heart. In fact, even sex with her is quite mechanical for him – devoid of any emotion, and forced.

Years pass by and Rohit, now a forty-two-years-old celebrated novelist, plays a great husband and a loving father to his seven-year-old daughter and six-year-old son. Yet he still feels empty inside, haunted by the thought that he is living a lie.

For some time, he wants to be by himself. He wants to be left alone. Hence, on the pretext of writing a unique book, he works out a solitary trip to Rajasthan.

In Rajasthan, he sets up his camp in the deep interiors of a magnificent desert. He spends his days all by himself, wandering through the scenic landscape. Until one fine day, he meets twenty-two-year-old Bhuvan, a boisterous but innocent Rajasthani village boy, who supplied goods to tourists camping in the interiors. Within a few interactions, a great bond develops between Rohit and Bhuvan. In Rohit, Bhuvan finds a comforting anchor, which could erase the wounds inflicted upon him by his tyrant father. And in Bhuvan's company, Rohit discovers his own cheerful, joyous and playful side. Their bond grow stronger with each passing day as Bhuvan becomes emotionally dependant on Rohit. While Rohit grows cheerier by the day.

In fact, as Rohit mails his drafts to his Publisher regularly, the Publisher is pleasantly surprised to see a brightness and excitement in his writing which was never there before. And as the bond between Rohit and Bhuvan grows to be stronger, for the first time, Rohit experiences the magical fascination of true love.

Initially, Rohit remains in denial about his need for intimacy with Bhuvan, despite several moments in which Bhuvan tries to be physically connected with him. But the more he resists, the more disturbed he feels. And there comes a point when he vents out his frustration on Bhuvan by shunning him away. He however realizes that staying away from Bhuvan was making him even more miserable.

Both are left languishing separately. Until one day, Rohit learns that Bhuvan was locked under police custody for a crime which was actually committed by his tyrant father. Forgetting all his apprehensions, Rohit goes to the police station and gets Bhuvan released and brings him to his camp.

That night, Bhuvan pours out all his pain about how he has always been tortured by his father. Rohit had never seen Bhuvan so vulnerable, so fragile, and so remorseful. Seeing Bhuvan crying, Rohit cannot keep away anymore.

And in order to give him some solace, Rohit wraps him in his arms.

At this delicate moment, Rohit and Bhuvan get swayed by their agony, and they drop all inhibitions and get lost in passionate love making. For the first time, Rohit experiences that sex could be so much more meaningful than just a physical act. Feelings which he had been deprived of all his life.

But then, reality strikes Rohit. He realizes that he has to put an end to this fairy tale and go back to his real world. And so, without informing Bhuvan, Rohit leaves Rajasthan.

However, once Rohit comes back to Mumbai, nothing seems to excite him anymore. He is persistently haunted by memories of Bhuvan. Everyone and everything around him seem pointless. Unable to contain his turbulent feelings, he once again traces out the clairvoyant Tushar for a private session.

Tushar tells him, "Bringing that boy here can spell disaster. You are a celebrity. And such things about celebrities don't remain hidden. It may ruin your image. And destroy your family. You are standing on the same crossroad where you were standing fourteen years earlier. And like I told you then, I say it again. If you want true love, which you have found in this boy, you will have to leave everything."

As his longing for Bhuvan keeps killing Rohit, day by day, his spirits keep sinking. Not much later, he slips into acute depression. No one around him is able to fathom the reason behind his depression.

Until, one day, Meghna chances upon his cell-phone. She sees video-recordings of Rohit with Bhuvan. She sees them playing, laughing, dancing and enjoying merrily. Meghna watches the recordings over and over. And ultimately, is convinced about Rohit's relationship with this boy.

After much soul-searching, Meghna walks up to Rohit and gently says, "I have never seen you as happy as you are with this boy. You have given so many years to all of us for our happiness. Now it is your turn to do something for yourself. Go where your happiness lies."

Rohit is overwhelmed by Meghna's graciousness. She goes to her children's room and holds the children tightly.

In the days that follow, Rohit transfers all his property, royalties from his writings, and all his wealth in Meghna's name. Just as he is about to leave, he asks her, "Will you ever be able to forgive me?"

"Forgive you for what?" Meghna replies. "You are the one who suffered the most"

In the magnificent deserts of Rajasthan, Bhuvan is sitting next to the river drowned in melancholy. Just then, his gaze falls upon a distant car. And in the car, he sees Rohit. Bhuvan is ecstatic. He runs like a maniac towards the car. Rohit walks up to him and grabs him in his arms. They get lost in a deep embrace and cry profusely.

THE END

THE ROAD TO FREEDOM

(Inspired by a poem 'Savitri ya Munnibai' by Dr. Sushma Sengupta)

Two women.

One a housewife and the other a prostitute.

Struggling with the same pain.

15 August 2009, 00:00 Hours. It's the time when the entire nation shall celebrate the 62nd anniversary of India's independence.

15 August 2009, 00:00 Hours. It's the time when the last train to Surajgarh leaves from Mumbai Central; the train in which Savitri's twelve-year-old daughter, Chanda, is being taken by her husband, Satyavan, to his native village to get her married to a thirty-five-year-old widower.

15 August 2009, 00:00 Hours. It's the time when the gate of builder Mangal Singh's bungalow is opened, the bungalow where Munnibai's thirteen-year-old daughter, Lali, is being taken by a local goon, Nandu, to meet the politician, Saawan Kher, as Lali's first step into the flesh trade.

At an age, when the Indian woman is claimed to be reaching the Sun, the Moon and the Stars, how have Chanda and Lali reached such an ugly state of extreme degradation and suffering?

To understand this, we go back in time into the story of Sagarpur, a basti in an obscure corner of Mumbai, inhabited by migrants from across the country – particularly from villages – in search of livelihood. Each one has his own life and his own stories and aspirations, yet they are all connected somewhere by abject poverty.

When Satyavan first moved into 'Kholi' in Sagarpur with his father and Savitri, he had stars in his eyes. The dream of working as a driver for a film star for a few years and then start his own car rental company. He wanted to conquer Mumbai.

Little did he know that Mumbai had already conquered him.

Thirteen years pass in his struggle for survival, a period when Savitri conceives and births four children, Chanda being the eldest of them. Yet Satyavan remains a driver. His dream sinks into alcoholism, his hopes buried into frustration. And the person who has to bear the brunt of all his bitterness was Savitri. Every night Satyavan returned home drunk, carrying the frustration of being treated as an inferior being by his employer, he vents out his frustrations by battering Savitri black and blue.

Savitri, simple and docile, could have been a beautiful woman. But the constant battering by her husband and the drudgery of multiple pregnancies at a young age, worsened by poor health and abject poverty, made her look frail and feeble and constantly worn-out.

The only brightness in her life came from her relationship with her children. Especially twelve-year-old Chanda – though still a child, her mother's pitiable existence left a strong impact on her. It ingrained a silent desire in her heart to one day to free her mother from the shackles of her circumstances.

'Freedom' for Savitri, however, did not exist. She had totally submitted to the pathetic situation she was living in. The only thing she silently craved for was her husband's love. She wanted to relive that moment when (during the first year of marriage) Satyavan used to put *sindoor* on her head and lovingly say, "I have stolen my wife from the moon."

But that could never happen because Satyavan had become bitter and frustrated, and she had become rusted. Her husband had lost all interest in her, which became even more apparent when Satyavan met the bright, spicy and always decorated woman, Munnibai, the foul mouthed, beedi smoking prostitute from the nearby brothel.

For Satyavan, Munnibai was a big relief, a great escape from his feelings of failure, which he felt when he was with the rest of the world, including his family. Finally, he had found someone of a status lower than his. Finally, he could pay for the pleasure devoid of being a reminder of great responsibilities. And finally, he could curse the world and in return get empathy, and in a pleasurable and cheerful way at that, for Munnibai always accepted his feelings, but never expressed her own. She knew she could never cross the line, never express how much she missed her family, for whom she entered into prostitution, and never go back to them for the same reason. She could never express the frustration of not being able to tell her thirteen-year-old daughter, Lali, who her father was, as she herself did not know. She could never express the suffocation of not being able to leave the brothel or else she and her daughter will be killed.

Hence, like Savitri, even for Munnibai, 'Freedom' did not exist. The only person who could sense her trauma was her daughter, Lali, who hopes that one day she would be able to do something to get her 'Freedom'.

So, the day Lali joins Chanda for a game of hopscotch, and they strike a friendship, they themselves do not know that it was beginning of a revolution. Chanda often playfully teases Lali for not knowing her father's name, a fact that always makes Lali ashamed. But she understands that Chanda was just being mischievous with no intension of demeaning her. Lali and Chanda become best of friends, regularly sharing their childish plans of how to rescue their respective mothers.

One day, they cajole Ramsaran, a school sweeper, to take them to the Govt. school where he worked. They had heard about the new exciting swings in the school playground. Also, this was the first time they would get to see a school, and more than the playground, it was the classroom which fascinated them greatly. With wonderous eyes they peep into a classroom through a window. As they intently watch, Keshav Dutt, the teacher in the classroom notices them.

At the first look, Keshav feels a strange connection with the two girls. Instead of scorning them, he asks them to come and sit inside the classroom. Chanda and Lali feel they had walked into a whole new world. At the end of the class, Keshav gives them a toffee, and a new relationship starts between Keshav and the two girls. With the greed for a toffee, they frequently attend Keshav's class, and eventually, the seed to rise in life is sown.

One day, as Keshav is teaching the students on great achievers of India, he shows the class a photograph of Simran Bedi. The picture of a woman in Police uniform has an overwhelming impact on Chanda and Lali. Suddenly, they seem to have found a breakthrough to their goal of liberating their mothers. Almost in unison, they tell Keshav, "I want to become Simran Bedi."

For Keshav, it is almost like time reversed. He is instantly haunted by a moment when he was ten years old and when his elder sister, Vimla, said, "I want to become a doctor." Keshav could see the same fire in Chanda and Lali's eyes.

Keshav's sister's dream got shattered in the hands of a dogmatic society. But this time, Keshav decides to help these girls accomplish their dream.

Meanwhile, Savitri and Munnibai are locked in a battle with each other without even having met each other. Having only heard about each other in bits from Satyavan, Savitri is jealous of Munnibai for being desirable to Satyavan, and Munnibai envies Savitri for holding a respectable status of his wife.

Craving to play the wife, whenever Satyavan comes, Munnibai offers him special dishes which she had cooked with her own hands, massages his legs, stitches his shirt buttons, stops using filthy language, gives up smoking beedi and when Satyavan is in need of money, she even manages to let him come to her without paying. Munnibai is completely lost in a false illusion which may crash anytime.

Savitri, on the other hand, makes all the efforts to look attractive. But despite all her efforts, Satyavan mocks and rejects her every time. In order to get money to buy clothes and jewellery, Savitri regularly goes to borrow money from the local Baniya Girdhari Lal, who is a lecherous lout. Savitri finds his indecent signals highly unsettling, but invariably her mission to win her husband makes her go to Girdhari for money. Somewhere down the line, Girdhari's 'Lust' for her starts getting overshadowed by a feeling of 'Pity' for her. And Savitri's 'disgust' for Girdhari starts getting replaced by a peculiar kind of 'respect' for him because he was the only man in the entire world who seemed to find her desirable.

Simultaneously, while Savitri and Munnibai's lives are confined to the basti, Satyavan is exposed to a much larger world – one of swanky cars and chic clothes, plush and snazzy multiplexes and hotels, grand shopping malls and sleek offices. Yet everything for him was beyond his reach.

One day his employer asks him to carry a bag of money to a person staying at the other end of the city. Even as Satyavan is carrying the bag, he is hammered by the fact that the bag contained so much money that if he grabs even half of it, he could start his own car rental company.

The temptation becomes too strong to resist. He ends up stealing thirty thousand rupees from the bag and delivers the rest to the concerned person without realizing the consequences. The matter escalates and Satyavan is put behind bars.

A desperate Savitri knocks every door in the basti and begs everyone to contribute for Satyavan's bail, but she finds only rebuttals everywhere. Finally, she surrenders to the last resort. She appeals to Girdhari for Satyavan's bail, willing to succumb to his lusty proposals.

That night, Girdhari calls Savitri to his godown. Savitri goes, nervous and fragile. As Girdhari comes close to her, she brings out a small box of *sindoor*. With closed eyes and great pain, she says, "Put this on my forehead and say 'I have stolen my wife from the moon'."

A sudden repentance and pity overwhelm Girdhari, robbing him of the strength to touch Savitri. He gives the money to Savitri and asks her to leave immediately. As she is leaving, Savitri asks, "Will you now stop praising me?"

Girdhari assures her that he will never stop appreciating her.

Meanwhile, as Satyavan is in police custody, Munnibai misses him greatly. As she is not allowed to step out of the brothel, the separation only makes her realize that she had fallen in love with Satyavan. Eventually, she shares her feelings for Satyavan with the brothel's local goon, Nandu, with whom she shares a friendly love-hate relationship.

At her behest, he takes her messages and food items for Satyavan to the police station, but he is not permitted to meet Satyavan as he himself has a criminal record and is on loggerheads with the police. But in order to keep Munnibai happy, Nandu always gives her a rosy picture and conveys false romantic messages from Satyavan to Munnibai, not realizing that he was only fuelling her illusions.

Thus, on the day Satyavan is granted bail and goes to see Munnibai, she holds on to Satyavan and begs him to take her and her daughter away with him. Satyavan is taken aback by Munnibai's first confession of her own plight. He is listless.

Once more his only pleasure was taking shape of a responsibility. He struggles to pacify her, but she is extremely persuasive. Ultimately, when she gets totally out of control, Satyavan slaps her and screams, "Bloody whore! Stay in your place. Don't try to become a wife!"

Satyavan's words shock Munnibai. In an emotional outburst, she cries, "A whore! That's all I mean to you. When I made you sweets, I was not a whore. When I massaged your back, I was not a whore. When I stitched your torn shirt, I was not a whore. But yes! At this moment I am a whore. And a whore knows only one language. Money. You have spent innumerable nights with me without paying me for them. Come back only when you have money to pay me for all those nights. And don't worry. I won't charge you for the emotions I gave you. Get lost!" Munnibai then violently shuns Satyavan away and holds Lali and cries profusely.

Keshav Dutt, meanwhile, steps on in order to get Chanda and Lali admitted to the school he was teaching in. But learning about Chanda's and Lali's backgrounds, he knows that he will have to convince a lot of people. As he talks to Chanda's family, he finds that they find girl's education was a total waste of time and money, and also blasphemous, as the inhabitants of Sagarpur basti hailed from remote villages of North India and still held a regressive mentality regarding women. For them, a girl's future was only to get married, produce children and stick to household work or menial jobs at best. Moreover, they believe emancipated women could be a threat to the authority of men in the community.

On the other hand, he is met by an equally vehement rejection from the brothel owners where Lali stays. The reason being brothel's 'Madam' Tara sees immense commercial prospects in Lali, and had already made promises to several customers who were waiting for Lali to blossom.

Keshav realizes that the only route to success could be awakening the very women who the girls had set goal for – Savitri and Munnibai. But there was no way he could get close to them. He needed a person who could motivate them on his behalf. After much searching, he finally finds someone who knew Savitri and Munnibai equally well.

Dr. Sadhna, who is practicing medicine from a small clinic in the basti has regular visits from both Savitri and Munnibai. Only Sadhna knew that though Savitri and Munnibai's lives seemed to be in sharp contrast with each other, they both were sailing in the same boat. In fact, she was prescribing the same medicines and diet to both of them. While Savitri could not afford the cost of treatment, Munnibai could not afford to have adequate rest for the treatment to work. Dr. Sadhna feels strongly for both the women, but finds herself helpless as she alone could not do anything more than merely giving the medical aid.

But the day Keshav approaches Dr. Sadhna to help him motivate Chanda and Lali's families to allow the girls join the school, Sadhna finds great support in Keshav. Hence, as Keshav and Sadhna join hands, the story of Sagarpur reaches a turning point.

They know that they will have to fight many battles before they could win the war. However, as they start confronting all odds, they realize that they were fighting a ruthless, indifferent and corrupt system.

On the exterior, Keshav has to struggle with insensitive school authorities, callous govt. employees and insensitive media, and in the interior, Sadhna finds it extremely difficult to convince Savitri to stand against her family and Munnibai to stand against the brothel. And while she endeavours to create awareness among the people of basti, she is confronted with vehement opposition by the old heads of basti, and is threatened by local goons of the brothel. She also faces opposition by the callous local police. Eventually her clinic is destroyed and she is abandoned by the basti.

Keshav, on the other hand, meets a similar fate and is suspended from his job. Yet, the two valiant crusaders do not let the fire in them die down. They cross all the barriers and reach the very person who unknowingly sparked off this fire – Simran Bedi.

In an intense emotional outburst, Keshav presents Chanda and Lali's case to Simran Bedi, who in turn is moved by it. She immediately instructs her junior inspector Vishal to look into the matter and give Keshav all the support he needed. Hence, with inspector Vishal, Keshav and Sadhna once again enter the basti.

But before this development, something dramatic has happened in Chanda's and Lali's lives.

Satyavan receives a marriage proposal from his native village for his thirteen-year-old daughter, Chanda, and that too for a thirty-five-year-old widower. In return the man has promised thirty thousand rupees to Satyavan to finally start a car rental company and break out from a life of misery and abject poverty.

Lured by the prospects, Satyavan accepts the offer. None of Savitri's desperate pleas can stop Satyavan, who has bought the train tickets for his native village. The train that will leave from Mumbai Central on 15 August at 00:00 Hrs.

Meanwhile, builder Mangal Singh has to clandestinely arrange 'entertainment' for his politician accomplice, Saawan Kher, at his bungalow. He sends his henchman Yadav to Sagarpur brothel to pick a girl who would suit Saawan's taste.

At the brothel, as Yadav looks at all the girls, Munnibai is aghast to see that he had selected Lali. All her protests are met with cold rebuttals. It is decided that the brothel's local goon, Nandu, will take Lali to Mangal Singh's bungalow, and would reach there by 00:00 Hrs. That is how Mangal Singh had planned to bring in the "Independence Day 2009".

14 August is the day when inspector Vishal reaches the basti with Keshav and Sadhna, but when the news of their reaching the basti reaches Satyavan, he quickly grabs Chanda and sneaks out of basti. He then takes her to his mechanic friend Jai kumar and hides her in his garage.

When Inspector Vishal reaches Satyavan's house, Satyavan's father tells him that Chanda had gone to her native village. Savitri, meanwhile, resigns to fate and stands silently.

Before leaving, Keshav tells her, "I know this is all a façade. I also know how much your daughter loves you. If you too love her just as much, gather strength from that love and save her from a life of suffering. Save her somehow and bring her to Shivaji Park in the evening. We will wait for you. You can do it. Your love can become the power to change your daughter's destiny."

Keshav leaves but his words keep haunting Savitri.

By the time Inspector Vishal, Keshav and Sadhna reach Tara's brothel, Lali has already been locked inside a cupboard. She is nowhere to be found and Vishal is told that there was no girl named Lali in the house. Even Munnibai, who has been threatened of dire consequences, claims that she never had a daughter.

Out of frustration Sadhna screams at Munnibai, "This is your only chance to save your daughter from becoming what you are. If you don't act now, she will be ridiculed by the society for her entire life. Do something! Do anything, but bring her to Shivaji Park in the evening. Only you can save your daughter! Only you!"

Sadhna leaves with Inspector Vishal and Keshav, but she has completely jolted Munnibai!

That night, as Nandu arrives to fetch Lali, Munnibai is also sent along with him to pacify her in case she throws any tantrums.

In the jeep, as Nandu drives, a defeated Munnibai says, "She has grown in front of your eyes. She has cried, played, danced in your arms. I never told you one thing – the day you got her ice-cream, she told me 'If I ever had a father, I wish he were like Nandu'."

Nandu doesn't react to Munnibai's words but his eyes reflect that he is deeply moved.

As they reach the point where Yadav and his men are waiting to receive Lali to take her to the bungalow, Yadav sleazily touches Lali and says, "Hope she is still a virgin."

Suddenly an enraged Nandu turns the jeep and drives away. Angered by Nandu's actions, Yadav and his men get into his car and follow Nandu.

Thus, a fiery chase starts with Nandu, Lali and Munnibai trying desperately to reach Shivaji Park.

The same evening, as Satyavan prepares to go to village, a defeated Savitri goes to borrow money from Girdhari. Looking at her distraught state, he says, "You look beautiful as ever."

Suddenly, Savitri breaks down. This is the first time Girdhari has seen her tears. He had no idea that it will be so unbearable for him to see her crying. As Satyavan goes to his friend's garage to fetch Chanda, he does not realize that Girdhari was following him in his lorry with Savitri sitting beside him.

As Satyavan brings out Chanda from the garage, Girdhari grabs Chanda and puts her on the lorry and drives away. In rage, Satyavan along with his mechanic friends get into a car and follow Girdhari's lorry.

Thus, a relentless chase starts as Girdhari, Savitri and Chanda try desperately to make it to Shivaji Park.

As from one direction, Savitri, from the other direction, Munnibai approach Shivaji Park, where on the eve of Independence Day, a celebration is being held, Simran Bedi, who is the event's Chief Guest, is giving an inspiring speech on 'Freedom'.

At the entrance, where Keshav and Sadhna are nervously waiting for Chanda and Lali to arrive, Savitri and Munnibai reach at the same time.

Satyavan with his friends and Yadav with his henchmen reach to nab Chanda and Lali, but the commotion is rattled when inspector Vishal intervenes.

Savitri presents Chanda and Munnibai presents Lali in front of inspector Vishal. As Vishal orders the negative forces to leave, Savitri requests him to pardon Satyavan and permit him to enter.

As they reach inside, Keshav and Sadhna are ecstatic. Keshav excitedly holds Chanda and Lali and takes them to the stage, interrupting Simran Bedi's speech. "These are the two girls I was talking about," he tells her. As Simran Bedi looks at them, Chanda and Lali are completely awestruck to see their idol right in front of their eyes.

Simran Bedi smiles at them and announces on the mike, "On this auspicious occasion of Independence Day Eve, I am happy to announce that my organization 'Aashajyoti' has decided to sponsor complete education and Police training of these two girls from Sagarpur." The entire crowd breaks into thunderous applause.

Keshav, Sadhna, Savitri, Munnibai, Nandu and Girdhari are unable to control their tears. And Satyavan, seeing his daughter on stage, finds his feelings of failure transforming into feeling of immense pride. On the stage, the anchor asks Lali to speak out her father's name on the mike. Once again, Lali feels ashamed and Munnibai deeply pained. Lali looks around the crowd where all the children were sitting with their fathers. She then raises her hand and points the finger at Nandu.

Nandu jumps in excitement, screaming, "I have become a father." Tears rush out of Munnibai's eyes.

Then, as Chanda is asked her father's name, Satyavan proceeds to rise from his seat proudly, Chanda looks at Satyavan intently and coldly says, "I don't know." Satyavan is stunned. An equally stunned Savitri rushes to the stage and cajoles Chanda to speak out her father's name, but Chanda continues claiming, "I don't know." Savitri starts beating Chanda and Sadhna rushes to the stage to control her. Completely overwhelmed with shock, Satyavan runs out of the ground. In utter frenzy, he starts running on the road like a possessed person. Flashes of all the atrocities he inflicted on Savitri and Munnibai hammer his mind. Finally, he collides with a tree and falls down. He cries, wails and screams in repentance, but there is no one there to hear his outburst.

On the other side, at 00:00 Hrs. sharp, Simran Bedi hoists the Indian flag with Chanda and Lali.

Years later, in a function, a bright Savitri is sitting in the audience with a pleasant looking Satyavan. She no more has the veil over her face. Instead, she has Satyavan's arm around her.

In some other corner, Munnibai is sitting next to Nandu. They both look the same as before. The only difference is that today Munnibai was wearing a *mangalsutra*.

In the function at the Police Academy, certificates are being awarded to now grown-up Chanda and Lali for completing their training as Police Officers. Once the ceremony is complete, they both excitedly come down from the stage and touch Keshav and Sadhna's feet.

Pictures of all Indian Women Achievers appear on screen as end credits roll.

THE END

CHAPTER FOUR

THE HEALING TOUCH

(in association with Nitin Tej Ahuja)

A relationship with no name, no identity.
A relationship too strong to deny, too intense to ignore.

Devika Narang had everything – a rich husband, a brilliant son, rows of servants, a group of social-bees for playing cards, regular high-profile parties, invitations to art exhibitions by celebrated artists, priority treatment at plush beauty parlours, a magnificent house, many sleek cars, expensive jewellery and designer clothes.

But then...

Deep inside, an uneasy feeling starts growing within Devika – a vacuum, a sense of being incomplete, of life being meaningless, of a lack of purpose. The more she indulged in her troubled feelings, more she felt that everything around her, about her, was meaningless.

And there was no one she could discuss her feelings with. Her husband Rajat Narang, living under the same roof, in pursuit of his professional accomplishments, had moved way beyond her for all practical purposes, making himself unavailable.

Her grown-up son Ashish, who in any case was disinclined towards connecting with her, had reached the age where he did not need or want parental attention anymore. She had everything. Still, she felt she had nothing. Not even herself.

One day, as a diversion from her regular socialite circle, Devika visits an old, forgotten friend, Shobhna Karat, who works as a Project Director in a reputed NGO. Being a sensitive person, Shobhna quickly notices Devika's inner turmoil and suggests Devika to get involved in some social work. According to her, there was nothing more fulfilling than to help out a person in distress. When Devika expresses her doubts, because she was not a trained social-worker, Shobhna suggests her to get involved in the project Shobhna was currently handling – the rehabilitation of earthquake victims shifted from Gujrat to Kalyan hospital in Mumbai. Shobhna says, "We have several earthquake victims in the hospital who are in need of help. They have been brought here for treatment and rehabilitation. Having gone through such a big upheaval, some of the patients are suffering from severe depression. The doctors are giving them medication and counselling, but what they also need is the company of someone who is not a medical professional. Someone who can be their friend. Someone who can empathize with them and who can provide them a listening ear. Will you like to be a volunteer, Devika? Will you like to be a Healer?"

That night, as Shobhna's words keep replaying in her mind, Devika looks around at all the material comforts she had in her home. She realizes that money cannot buy everything. She also reviews her relationship with her husband and son, which somewhere down the line had slipped out of her hands in a seemingly irreversible manner.

The next day, Devika meets Shobhna at Kalyan Hospital and offers her services as a volunteer. Shobhna asks her to attend a particular patient, but warns her that she would need to have a great deal of patience, tolerance and of course, lot of compassion and understanding.

Thus, Devika meets Vikram Shah.

In the earthquake, Vikram has lost his entire family. His business too is completely wrecked as his factories in Gujrat have been reduced to debris. He has been brought to this hospital in a critical state for rehabilitation. Some distant relatives and friends did pay him customary visits, but besides offering empty condolences, they showed no intention to accommodate him in their lives.

At the beginning, Devika finds Vikram in a terrible condition – bedridden with multiple fractures, depressed, quiet, constantly staring into nothing, without sleep, without food, without medicines. But when he does respond to Devika's efforts, it is only in the form of bitterness towards her kindness; he rejects her efforts with caustic remarks, demanding to be left alone. He lashes out, saying, "I know what you high-society birds are all about. You just want to brag in your social circles about what a great work you are doing. About giving time to a helpless man. Because charity is fashionable for you. Something you flaunt. But you won't do it at my cost. I don't need your generosity. Get lost!"

Devika feels frustrated, helpless and even angry. But when she tells Shobhna about her feelings, Shobhna says, "Take this case as a challenge. After all, what is life without a challenge?"

Thus, Devika continues tending to Vikram with renewed enthusiasm. And yes. Slowly, with her continued dedication despite all his bitterness, Vikram begins to get used to her presence and even starts responding to her empathy for him.

He starts confiding into her – he shares memories of his loving family and friends, those he had lost in the earthquake, whom he had seen getting crushed to death with his own eyes.

Whenever he sheds tears, Devika assures him that one day, with positive efforts, he will get over the pain and remember his loved ones with a smile on his face. Devika's support becomes a huge motivator for Vikram and his life finds colours of some bright moments.

One day Devika motivates him to get up and he sits up for the first time. Another day, he sits on the wheel-chair, and Devika takes him outside to see the sky, the greenery, the peacocks. And finally, comes the day he starts walking.

For Devika, it was not just Vikram's recovery, it was also an achievement for her.

Vikram always thanked her for bringing him back to life. But in her heart, she knew that she had to thank Vikram too, because it was due to him that she could feel important, worthy. Otherwise, whatever she did for her husband and son was always taken for granted and never got any praise, respect or even acknowledgement. For them, she was just performing her duties. Whenever, out of excitement, Devika told her family about how she was appreciated in the hospital, her husband's reaction was so mild and indifferent that Devika decided not to share her achievements with anyone at home.

Finally, the day comes when Vikram is discharged from the hospital. Fortunately, Vikram has an account in a local bank with a decent amount of funds. With the help of some of these funds, Devika gets Vikram a flat.

Living in the new flat, the homely environment makes Vikram feel a great longing for his lost home. To help him with it, Devika puts in all the efforts to pacify him – she cooks for him like his wife did, she plays chess with him like his children did. And in return, Vikram is full of gratitude – something that was so precious for Devika.

But then, things changed.

When in hospital, Devika's hourly visits were enough for the day for Vikram since there were other people to help out too. But now, with no one else around, Vikram started needing Devika even more. Whenever she was not there, his loneliness and memories start haunting him. As a result, he starts demanding more and more time from Devika. But however much she tries, her duties at home like attending important parties with her husband, entertaining her son's guests, looking after the daily functioning of the house always called for her, making it increasingly difficult for her to manage.

One day, on Devika's birthday, during her regular visit to Vikram's house, she is met by a surprise. Vikram has decorated his living room and even organized a candle-light dinner to celebrate Devika's birthday. Although Devika is very happy, she hesitantly tells Vikram that she couldn't stay back for dinner. Instead, she invites Vikram to the birthday party organized at her place.

Though initially sceptical, Vikram agrees to go. In the evening, as Vikram comes to the party, a sudden realization strikes him. He sees that Devika had a vast world besides him. She has a husband, a son, friends and colleagues. Vikram realizes that he was just a small part of Devika's life... just an object for social service for Devika. Nothing more. Dejected and heartbroken, Vikram comes home and lies down on the floor, still and frozen.

Next day, when Devika comes, she gets extremely panicky when Vikram refuses to reply or even open the door. Finally, she calls Shobhna who gets some helpers to break open the door, only to find Vikram lying inside like a lifeless object.

Shobhna analyses the situation and advises Devika that she should withdraw herself and try to stay away from Vikram for some time as he had become too dependent on her. On not doing so, the whole purpose of making him a complete and independent individual would be lost.

Following Shobhna's advice, Devika stops going to Vikram's house, even when she is pained to realize that compared to Vikram's need for her, her own 'need to be needed' had become much stronger.

Shobhna, meanwhile, explains to Vikram that Devika had distanced from him for his own well-being, and that he needed to be strong and not make anybody his crutches. Later, through her, Vikram meets other earthquake victims – an old woman suddenly left on her own without any support, an old man succumbed to immense loneliness, a young boy crumbling under shattered dreams, and more such hopeless lives.

For the first time, Vikram is overwhelmed to realize that he was not alone in this tragedy. And that there were others too suffering losses, probably more than he had to, with no one to turn to.

Deeply moved by their predicament, a sudden surge of positive spirit overcomes Vikram and he motivates everyone to join hands, to create a common goal, something which would erase their wounds and make them move forward and even give them a reason to live. Hence, the seed of a small showroom of Gujrati handicrafts is sown.

With great enthusiasm, Vikram with his team relentlessly works towards realizing his dream, ushering in a phase that fosters a great amount of togetherness coloured with several poignant and cheerful moments, unknowingly creating a loving family.

All this while, Devika keeps herself abreast with Vikram's activities through Shobhna. Staying in the background, she supports him in every way she could – whether it was arranging for raw materials at discounted rates or even organizing loans for his showroom – for Vikram's progress gave Devika a personal sense of achievement.

Finally, the auspicious day of the showroom's inauguration arrives. There is a feeling of immense joy and pride in the air. Amidst this merriment, Vikram notices Shobhna arriving to attend the inaugural ceremony. As

Vikram greets her, he is met with a great surprise.

Devika has come with Shobhna. Shobhna tells Vikram, "Today you have become truly independent. Now I will never stop Devika from meeting you."

Meeting Vikram after a long time, Devika is extremely happy to see him in his new persona – bright, confident and positive. And Vikram gives the entire credit for his growth to Devika. He announces, "Whatever I am today is because of one person. The person who, with her positive spirit, has gifted me a second life. Devika Narang."

The whole showroom resounds with a hearty applause for Devika.

As Vikram makes her light the lamp for the inaugural ceremony, she feels immensely honoured. She had finally got what she had always been feeling devoid of – self-worth.

Later, Devika suggests Vikram to introduce the concept of producing Gujrati handicrafts to more people in Gujrat who have been affected by the earthquake by spreading awareness and motivating people all over Gujrat.

The idea seems interesting to Vikram, but he is not sure whether he will be able to pursue it all alone. Without giving it a second thought, Devika volunteers to join him in the endeavour. As Devika prepares to go for her Gujrat trip, her family is least concerned. In fact, no one even asks her when she would be back. Being in a home, she didn't have a family, while Vikram now has many people showering love and affection upon him. Being all alone, he had created a family.

During their trip to various villages of Gujrat, along with holding Awareness Programs, Vikram and Devika share many beautiful experiences together, and a growing fondness makes them feel closer than ever before.

On the last day of the Awareness Campaign, a large number of people have gathered at a ground. These are the people who have enlisted for Vikram's project and are here to take an oath that through this project they will stand on their own feet and will help others do so too.

Each person holds the hand of the person adjoining him or her forming an endless chain as everyone takes the oath. In this process, Devika and Vikram happen to hold each other's hands. There is a great poignancy and strong under-currents between them at the physical touch. They continue holding hands even though the oath has been taken. Each waiting for the other to release the grip. Finally, they reluctantly disengage their hands. This is the first sign of romance, first brush with intimacy between them and also a clear indication that from now on, they could not relate to each other as before. Nor they could take their relationship any further.

In the interactions that follow, neither Vikram nor Devika utter a word about their restless hearts. However, their silences speak volumes about their inner turbulence.

By the time Devika proceeds to come back to Mumbai, Vikram diffidently informs her that he had decided to continue staying in Gujrat as he felt he needed to do much more work there. But Devika knows where his decision came from. While parting, Devika sombrely asks, "Can't we be friends?"

Vikram honestly replies, "May be sometime in future. But at present, we should be nothing."

Broken-hearted Devika and Vikram part ways, with no promises of a reunion.

In Mumbai, holding on to Vikram's memories, Devika once again adopts a lifestyle which no more gave her pleasure. Her shimmering socialite persona reflects a consistent streak of sadness which she tries to conceal behind a fake smile.

Vikram, on the other hand, is constantly struggling in Gujrat with the vacuum left by Devika. To help distract himself, he gets involved in the welfare of quake victims by setting up handicrafts shops for them.

Eventually, Vikram starts getting attention from the media for his noble efforts. With the image Vikram assumes in public eye, big opportunities couldn't be far. And the golden opportunity did knock at his door. Rashtriya Jan Sangh, a national-level political party, invites him to join the party and contest in the elections.

Though he is reluctant, the Party Chief Damodar Rao convinces him that being a political leader will give him powers to pursue his noble cause in a much better and bigger way. Thus, Vikram's life turns a new leaf even as Devika's life goes back to where it was –stagnant, mundane and meaningless.

The only bright moment that enlivens Devika's spirits after a long time comes when Devika chances upon watching Vikram's interview on television right after he has won the elections. She is even more elated to learn that Vikram was making a short trip to Mumbai in accordance with his political programs. She is sure that Vikram will go out of the way to meet her. Little does she realize that while her world has remained the same, Vikram's world had changed drastically. He was no more the lonely man living an isolated and idle existence. Today, he had innumerable people and countless tasks in his life in which Devika had no place.

As Devika anxiously looks forward to Vikram's arrival at the airport, there are hundreds of others waiting too. Once Vikram arrives, Devika struggles to tear through the crowd to reach Vikram, but she fails and is left disappointed watching Vikram leave with his party workers. Devika makes more attempts to connect with Vikram, but is still unsuccessful. But the most hurting part was that Vikram had not made any effort to meet her.

For Vikram, who is completely engrossed in fulfilling his pre-scheduled engagements, thoughts about Devika do cross his mind like a flash, but his memory chain is invariably broken by the people and events around him, leaving no space to think about her.

Finally, by coincidence, Devika happens to be in a party where Vikram too arrives. While everyone struggles to gain his attention, Devika makes no such attempts. As Vikram spots her standing in a corner, he walks up to her and initiates a poignant conversation, he realizes that somewhere down inside, she felt hurt that he had completely forgotten her. Vikram asks her out for a walk in the garden, where Devika confesses, "You are so occupied, unapproachable, inaccessible. I know it is wrong for me to feel this way, but the fact is I am missing the days you wanted me to be with you all the time."

Vikram understands Devika's feelings and gently says, "Don't worry. Come what may, I'll talk to you every day. Every single day. And all the days I am here, I shall meet you. Today, we can be friends, can't we?"

Vikram's words soothe Devika's heart. And the next few days, whatever little time she gets to spend with Vikram, is most fulfilling for her.

But this beautiful dream does not last for long.

That day, as Vikram gets ready to leave for his meeting with Devika, he is taken aback to find Damodar Rao in the Party Guest house. Damodar appears highly disturbed. He shows Vikram an article published in a leading magazine which had pictures of Vikram and Devika in various places. The article was written in a highly sensational manner with the title "Secret connection with a married woman."

Vikram is taken aback. He tells Damodar that Devika was a good friend and a very nice woman. But Damodar insists that in order to protect his public image, he should stop meeting Devika with immediate effect.

Vikram softly yet adamantly replies, "I am sorry. This is not possible."

Damodar makes him realize that if not for his own sake, he should break this connection for the sake of the woman he cared for so much, as this relationship will not only tarnish her image in society, it would also ruin her marital life and her family.

Deeply concerned about Devika, a disheartened Vikram succumbs to the demand of circumstances.

At Devika's house, a commotion is taking place in the lobby of the first floor. Her son Ashish is screaming at the top of his voice, "My friends, my colleagues, all were making fun of me. Relatives are calling. How could you do such a disgusting thing?"

In a huff, as Ashish leaves, Rajat softly yet very bitterly tells Devika, "Whatever you want to do with your life, I have no objection. But please... please don't destroy my reputation. Don't try to make your path by blocking mine."

Without giving her a chance to explain, Rajat leaves too. Devika is left languishing all alone in agony. Never before had she felt so fragile, so weak.

Hence, the moment she receives a letter from Vikram, she grabs it as if this was her only support. In the letter, Devika reads, "I don't want you to suffer because of me. It will be best for both of us that we do not keep any hopes of meeting anymore. Believe me, wherever I am, I'll keep praying for your happiness every moment. Goodbye."

Devika is completely shattered. She realizes her relationship with Vikram had ended, finished, destroyed within seconds. Just like an earthquake. Breaking down, shedding tears, she cries uncontrollably, with no one to console her.

Meanwhile, Vikram enters his home and straight away heads for his room, ignoring Damodar Rao who has been waiting for him. In his room, Vikram tries to muster up as much courage as he could, but he is not able to control himself from shedding tears.

Noticing this, Damodar tries to pacify him, "Be strong. In their life, politicians have to make many sacrifices. Most of them are such that they are not even noticed by others. This is just a small sacrifice. The first step towards accepting the fact that now you are a public-property."

From here on, Vikram devotes himself completely to politics. He works day and night, rising from success to success. He has everything, except a personal life. Yet, he has half an hour every day, before he goes to sleep, which he keeps only for himself. During this time, he writes letters to Devika sharing the whole day's experiences. "Devika, I'm sure you are doing well. You have always been a positive person. Nothing can keep you down for long." Every day, without fail, he writes a letter. But he never posts the letter.

However, Devika's life is not as positive as Vikram imagines to be. The loss of Vikram has taken its toll on her. Her emotional downfall started the moment she realized he was gone. She becomes a gloomy, lifeless person, something which is met by cold indifference by Rajat and Ashish. Devika had become emotionally numb.

Finally, Devika is shown to a psychiatrist. He concludes that Devika was suffering from acute depression. If not treated promptly, the consequences could be serious. He says one of the family members had to be with her all the time and she could not be left alone.

Rajat says that he will be visiting Germany, France, Switzerland and US over the next six months on a business assignment which he cannot avoid at any cost. Ashish angrily says, "Don't look at me. I don't know how to handle her. Moreover, I can't leave everything and sit next to her."

Ultimately, Rajat suggests that Devika be admitted in the VIP ward of the hospital where she can be under constant medical supervision. The expenses obviously were no problem. Dr. Kapoor has to succumb to this last option and Devika is shifted to the hospital.

In the following days, Devika spends her time staring into space with forlorn eyes in her hospital private ward, engulfed by severe depression. Once in a while, Shobhna pays her a visit, only to be saddened to learn that with each passing day, Devika's condition was deteriorating further.

On the other side, Vikram rises from success to success in his role as a politician. But none of his feats in politics are able to eliminate the persistent remorse in his eyes. Damodar notices this, but he chooses to ignore it no matter much concerned he is for Vikram.

The day arrives when Damodar's party has organized a grand function in an auditorium in Gujrat. The purpose of this function is to felicitate individuals and organizations who have given commendable contribution towards earthquake relief. In this context, Shobhna too is invited to the function. During the break, Vikram spots Shobhna and walks up to her. The initial formal conversation eventually becomes informal, leading to the topic of Devika.

Shobhna informs, "Actually, Devika is not too well."

Concerned Vikram asks what had happened to Devika.

Shobhna replies "acute depression. You would understand. The same condition you had been in. In fact, she is admitted in a hospital. Her family has in a way abandoned her. She has no one by her side. I am afraid, if she continues deteriorating the way she is, she may not survive for long. Vikram, you were lucky that Devika entered your life as a healer. Unfortunately, Devika does not have any such healer."

Hearing this, Vikram is overcome with a sudden storm of emotions. Nothing except Devika seems significant anymore. Immediately, Vikram instructs his subordinates to cancel all his appointments. Their pleas about the importance of the commitments are met with deaf ears. He asks his driver to rush to his guest house where he starts packing his bags.

By this time, the news had reached his head office and he started getting frantic calls from his seniors. But he simply refuses to obey their orders. Disconnecting all phone calls on his way, he rushes to the airport and catches the first flight to Mumbai. There is total commotion amongst party members regarding his whereabouts. Only Damodar stands quietly in contemplation, and at one point, he instructs his party members, "Don't follow him. Let him go. He will not be here. He was never here."

On reaching Mumbai, Vikram directly heads for the Hospital, where he anxiously asks for Devika's ward and rushes to see her.

Finally, Vikram enters the ward. He is deeply hurt to see frozen Devika sitting, staring into vacant space. As he calls her name, she looks at him as if not trusting her own eyes. For a few moments, overwhelmed Devika and Vikram just look at each other soulfully. Then, in a broken voice, Vikram says, "What have you done to yourself? You were never like this. You were the one who taught me to be positive, strong and happy. No. I won't let you be like this. I have to be with you. All the time. I don't care what the world thinks, what the society says. All I know is that I have to be with you."

Then, he takes out a bundle of letters and hands it over to her and says, "I said I will talk to you every day. This is the proof that I didn't go back on my words."

As Devika glances through the letters, tears start flowing from her eyes and she is unable to control herself from crying.

Vikram pleads, "No. Stop crying. You were not like this. Stop it or else I shall go back right now."

Devika replies, "No. You will not go anywhere. You will stay here and see me cry. I have saved all these tears for this moment. Only for this moment."

Devika breaks all the barriers and embraces Vikram tightly and cries profusely. Vikram too puts his arms around her to provide her solace. All this while they were holding back, but in this moment, they realize they need no one more than each other, opening their hearts completely, holding each other tightly. Devika and Vikram cry and cry and cry.

THE END

CHAPTER FIVE

MERCEDES

In the disparity between haves and have-nots,
one poor couple dares to live a dream.

Twenty-six-year-old Vishal has arrived Mumbai Central railway station with his newly wedded wife, Rashmi. Back home in the village, Raigarh, Vishal is a farmer who works along with his father. After one month of marriage, Vishal has brought his wife Rashmi to show Mumbai.

They get a place to stay in Vishal's childhood friend Chandu's house. It is a small, unkempt room in a *chawl*. As such Vishal and Rashmi have no big dreams. They are content to survive on the paltry sum that Vishal earns through farming in the village. However, after coming to Mumbai they realize that probably their village is not the right place for them to spend their lives. High-rise buildings, colourful lights, magnificent beaches, plush cinema halls, impressive restaurants and smooth roads simply make Vishal and Rashmi fall in love with Mumbai. Thus, Vishal decides not to return to Raigarh. Instead, he would find a job in Mumbai. Rashmi supports Vishal's decision. She is quite excited with the idea of living in a vibrant city.

With Chandu's help, Vishal gets a job as a driver of a well-to-do businessman, Ranbir Mathur. The car Vishal is supposed to drive is a swanky Mercedes. When Vishal is not driving Ranbir around, he is supposed to take Ranbir's wife Madhu for shopping and pick up his children from the school. Thanks to the job, Vishal shifts into a small *kholi* with Rashmi.

Being new to Mumbai, he is often scolded for taking wrong routes. He is scolded for not washing the car properly. He is scolded for not checking the tyre pressure regularly. Vishal, like a sissy, swallows all the scolding, nasty comments and caustic remarks without retaliation. And later, he consoles himself by thinking that after all it was 'his' fault for which he got scolded. Otherwise, Ranbir and his family were not heartless people. They were always concerned about Vishal's welfare, asked him whether he had had food, whether he slept properly in the night etc.

Since the Mathurs often went for late night parties, Vishal has to be on duty till very late, most of the times till around two-o-clock in the night. At such times, obviously there are no buses plying. Vishal has no way to go to his kholi, which is quite far. Once Ranbir comes to know about this problem, he asks Vishal to take the car with him and bring back the next morning as he comes on duty.

Taking the car home becomes almost a routine affair for Vishal. Every night, as Vishal comes back from duty, he takes Rashmi out for a drive. This drive becomes the only entertainment, relaxation and excitement of their lives. They regularly go to the *cycle-wallah* at Juhu who sells coffee. During these times, the sissy attitude of Vishal vanishes. He behaves like the owner of the car. His mannerism automatically becomes commanding and authoritative.

Nevertheless, all such trips are not tension-free. There are few incidents, which bring danger too. Once Vishal is hauled by police for over speeding. The policeman demands the car owner's phone number. Vishal is in a fix. Finally, Rashmi pleads with the policeman and with much difficulty, he lets them go. In another incident, an auto rickshaw bangs into the car and makes a small dent in the car. Vishal is petrified to imagine Ranbir's reaction once he sees the dent. To nervous Vishal's utter surprise, Ranbir's reaction is very mild. He simply asks Vishal to get the dent repaired.

Gradually, the car becomes the most important thing in Vishal and Rashmi's life. Every night, as it is past 12, Rashmi starts getting dressed up to go out. In fact, unlike other wives, Rashmi hopes that Vishal has long duty hours so that he can get the car home.

On the work front, Vishal takes Ranbir to his office, hotels and the business conferences. As he sees these posh buildings and high-class lifestyle, a feeling of deprivation creeps in Vishal. On the other hand, Madhu often calls Rashmi as an additional help whenever there was a party at home. As Rashmi serves the guests, she is enamoured by the expensive cutlery, splendid crockery and luxurious furniture of the house. And suddenly, the feeling of deprivation creeps into Rashmi too. As the feeling of deprivation keeps aggravating, a new feeling takes birth in their hearts. A feeling that was never there before – aspiration.

"What wrong have we done? The same God as theirs has also created us. How come they have so much and we have nothing? Absolutely nothing? Everything is so near yet so far! We don't possess a single thing, which can bring us happiness. Not a single thing," says Vishal. Suddenly, Vishal takes a look at the car. The Mercedes. By his expression, Rashmi comes to know what was in Vishal's mind. Then and there, without giving it a second thought, Vishal and Rashmi decide to steal the car. It's late in the night when Vishal and Rashmi dump all their belongings into the car and drive away. Away from the city of contradiction, between deprivation and affluence. They realize that the safest place to go to is their own village.

Strange incidents occur as they drive towards their village. On the way, they find a bus, which has just broken down. One of the passengers halts the car and asks for a lift. Vishal says the lift will cost him two-hundred rupees. The man finds it quite strange that the owner of a Mercedes should be asking for a petty sum of two-hundred rupees for a lift. He is perplexed. As he is about to sit in the car, he calls his family to join him. To Vishal and Rashmi's shock, the man has an incredibly obese wife and 6 fat children. They all get stuffed in the car. While traveling, the so-called kids create havoc in the car. One is fiddling with the music system while other is scratching the window and one is spilling juice all over. Finally, they are dropped at their destination, much to Vishal and Rashmi's relief.

After a while, they find another man halting the car for a lift. He offers five-hundred rupees for a lift. Tempted by the offer and seeing him alone, Vishal takes him in. But minutes later, siren of a police jeep is heard. Vishal and Rashmi are flabbergasted. Vishal increases the speed of the car as police follows the car. A wild chase takes place as Vishal tries his best to escape. Finally, the police jeep manages to halt the car. Vishal and Rashmi are petrified. Just as the police comes near them, a surprise knocks them. It's not them whom the police had been looking for. Instead, they were chasing the man who took lift in their car. Apparently, he was a criminal. Vishal tells the police that he was dodging the police because the man had threatened to kill him if he doesn't do as he says. As the police arrest the man and take him away, Vishal and Rashmi thank their stars.

But another question props up in their minds. What will they tell the family, the neighbours and the community? What impression will they get once they come to know that it was a stolen car? Suddenly, Vishal comes up with a freaky idea. He detaches the AC, music system, side mirrors and other accessories of the car and proceeds to sell them. Once he sells these things, he gets enough money on his hands to buy new clothes, shoes, etc.

Vishal and Rashmi reach their village in a car which they claim is theirs. Vishal tells everybody that he has a sprawling business in the city. Vishal projects a high-class attitude and Rashmi too, adorns a hoity-toity demeanour. Their stay in the village is full of fun. Vishal becomes the pride of the village. Rashmi gets immense respect from the ladies of the village.

Finally, the day comes when Vishal's money gets over. Vishal decides to go to city. Rashmi convinces him that it was risky to go to Mumbai. Hence, Vishal and Rashmi drive down to Delhi.

In Delhi, Vishal gets a job of a cleaner in an arts exhibition center. The first problem is that Vishal needs a place to stay and he does not have the money for that. Vishal and Rashmi discuss the problem and find that the only solution is to sell the car. It is a too big a decision. By now they had got emotionally attached to the car. Vishal strikes a deal with a garage owner. The day the garage owner is supposed to take away the car, Rashmi is totally broken. It appears as if all their happy times were about to come to an end. Realizing he will never be able to see Rashmi that happy again, at the last moment, Vishal changes his decision and refuses to sell the car. Rashmi instantly brightens up. Vishal and Rashmi decide to make the car itself their home. In the subsequent days, Vishal and Rashmi get quite used to sleeping in the car and life seems pretty content for them. Little do they know that Ranbir had complained to the police about Vishal and that police were searching for him.

One day, Vishal asks Rashmi to come and visit the exhibition hall he was working in. When Rashmi comes, she is aghast to see the prices of the paintings exhibited. Later, an idea strikes Rashmi. She buys some colours and starts painting pictures on the car. In a few days, as Vishal went to work, Rashmi keeps herself occupied by beautifying the car. On the other side, Ranbir is making preparations for a business conference he has to attend in Delhi.

One morning, as Vishal wakes up, he finds Rashmi doing pooja in front of the car. When he enquires about the occasion, she tells him that it was their car's anniversary. One year back, Vishal had brought this car home for the first time. Vishal asks Rashmi to be ready in the evening. Once he comes back from work, they both will go somewhere and celebrate.

It's a happy day for Vishal. He is unusually excited. As the exhibition starts, one man taps Vishal to ask the directions to the exhibition hall. As Vishal turns, he is stunned. The man is none other than Ranbir. Immediately Vishal starts to run away. On the other hand, Ranbir informs the police. Vishal comes running to Rashmi, who is all decked up for the celebration, and makes her sit in the car. By the time Vishal starts the car, he sees a police jeep approaching him.

A massive chase takes place in which Vishal tries his best to dodge the police.

Ultimately Vishal gets caught. The car which Rashmi and Vishal loved so dearly is taken away from them.

Now, Vishal is about to be labelled a criminal. Rashmi begs Ranbir to forgive Vishal as once he has a criminal record, he will not get a job anywhere. But Rashmi's pleas are unheard by Ranbir.

As the police is taking Vishal to the police van, he turns and takes a last look at the car. His feelings get out of control and he pushes aside the policemen and madly, wildly and violently breaks the car. By the end of it, the car is shattered. As the policemen hold him, Vishal breaks down and cries profusely.

Rashmi comes to Vishal and wipes his tears. She softly says, "Enough. Now everything will be all right. Now we will never look at a car again. Once you come out of prison, we will go to our village. For us, our bullock cart is the best. Everything will be fine."

With the promise of a better tomorrow, Vishal waves goodbye to Rashmi.

THE END

CHAPTER SIX

SPOTLIGHT

A film-star's battle with himself.

Tonight, Mikhil's excitement knows no bounds. He is getting ready to go for what is by far the biggest event of Superstar Ronit Khera.

Ronit Khera.

Mikhil had grown up watching his films, emulating him as much as he could, and going by whatever information he grasped about Ronit from magazines and television channels, Mikhil started worshipping Ronit Khera as the ultimate star, the ideal hero and his greatest inspiration. No wonder, Mikhil aspires to make it as an actor in movies with a single-minded goal – to one day become a Superstar as big as Ronit, and achieve all the fame, name, wealth and success which stardom brings.

Tonight, he enthusiastically looks forward to watch his idol performing on stage and plans to cheer Ronit with uncontrolled adulation while sitting in the audience.

However, Mikhil's craving for stardom finds little approval from his mother who keeps prodding him to give up his crazy dream and help his father in running his opticians store. According to her, his father was getting old and needed Mikhil to support him. Because of this, even tonight, Mikhil has landed up in a heated argument with his mother. As usual, the altercation does not reach any conclusion, and Mikhil storms out of the house abruptly.

Though he is agitated by his squabbles with his mother, his entire bitterness vanishes the moment he reaches the event venue. Ronit Khera's picture is splashed all across the massive stadium – on posters, hoardings, cut-outs, standees and brochures.

Mikhil, like everyone else in the audience, gets increasingly desperate to see his hero, his idol, his superstar on stage. And as time passes, the eagerness in the audience gets more and more intensified. Two hours had passed since the show began, there have been some insignificant dance performances. But Ronit Khera has not appeared on stage till now.

The audience's patience is running out. Unable to contain their patience anymore, the crowds start screaming and chanting Ronit's name. As the entire stadium resounds with cries of a restless audience, they do not know that something chaotic is brewing in the background.

They do not know that Ronit Khera is missing!

In a hush-hush manner, to avoid any kind of media uproar, the organizers have started a frantic search for Ronit. But he is nowhere to be found. He is neither at home, nor at his regular hangouts. His phones are switched off. His friends and relatives have no clue about his whereabouts. On the top of that, even his Manager Kirti is not taking any phone calls.

Sitting at a friend's place, Kirti watches the live coverage of the show looking extremely tensed. After a while, she gets a phone call which she simply cannot avoid, as the call is from none other than Ronit.

In a broken voice, he asks her, "Did you reach the stadium?"

Kirti agonizingly replies, "No Ronit. I can't do this."

Ronit says, "You are my friend, aren't you? I have never asked you for anything. Can't you do this much for me? This is the first and last time I am asking you to do something for me. As a true friend."

Ronit's words leave Kirti completely distraught. Gathering as much courage as she could, she proceeds for the stadium.

When Kirti reaches the stadium in a highly jittery state, the organizers pounce upon her with a thousand questions about Ronit's absence. Finally, unable to control anymore, she reveals, "He is not coming."

Everyone around her is startled. They attack her with more questions, not knowing how to pacify the agitated audience.

To this, Kirti volunteers, "I will talk to the audience."

Putting up a brave front, Kirti comes on the stage and announces, "With heartfelt apologies, I have to say, that Ronit Khera will not be here with us."

Kirti's words leave audience absolutely enraged. It becomes impossible to handle the fury. Kirti continues to hold on to the mike somehow and announces, "Friends, I have a recording which Ronit wants you to watch. I know nothing can compensate his absence, but I beg you to watch this recording. Because this may be the last time you will get to see him."

Suddenly, the audience is left dumbstruck. A stony silence takes over the entire stadium. And in this eerie silence, the video recording which Kirti had carried with her is played. In few seconds, Superstar Ronit Khera appears on each and every screen.

All cameras from various television channels are directed towards the screens and the entire nation seems to be watching Ronit's address to his fans, in a sombre tone, he says, "Friends, all through these years, I have touched you through many stories, many characters. Many of you have loved me, many of you have worshipped me and many of you want to become like me. But the fact is, the Ronit you know is just a marketing product, a brand. Not the real me. Because I was neither given a chance, nor did I have the guts to show you what I really am. I can't say why, but today I have this intense urge to share with you *my* story, *my* character. The Ronit you have always loved, but one you have never known."

Elsewhere, in a dark, deserted valley, a car sits parked at a cliff with one man sitting alone inside it. This man is Ronit Khera, looking broken, unnerved, consuming high doses of cocaine.

As a panic-stricken search for Ronit continues, a distressed Ronit on the screen tells is audience about his journey, even as Ronit, in reality, is sitting inside the car, consuming more and more cocaine.

Ever since he remembered, Ronit had wanted to become a star, for he had an extraordinarily rosy picture of stardom. He truly believed that once he becomes a star, all the happiness in the world will be at his feet. With this desire, he struggled his way through the ups and downs on the path to success. And with the first film itself, Ronit tasted instant stardom. After that, there was no looking back, one hit after another, one award after another and with an ever-growing deluge of fans, he was undoubtedly the youngest superstar in the history of Indian Cinema.

Ruling the film industry and millions of hearts, he got name, fame, wealth and success in abundance. But somewhere down the line, the one thing he lost was his peace of mind.

The first reality which had befallen upon him was that being a star, he had become a public property, and that the entire world had the right to pass judgments on him. Every good or bad remark he came across in magazines, newspapers, television channels or amongst masses strongly affected him. His happiness or disgruntlement got monitored by opinions of others. He thought he ruled millions, but in reality, he had become a slave of millions. So much so that wherever he went, whatever he said, whatever he did, he came under constant scrutiny. Every part of his being - how he walks, how he talks, whom he meets, what he eats, what he wears – was being noticed and evaluated by public and media. He was so confined to a fixed image that others appreciated that even a small change like a different hair cut made him highly conscious.

What's more, there was an overbearing pressure to maintain his success at the same level. He had to live in killing anxiety as he had to prove his worth again and again. Every new film had to be as big or bigger hit than the previous one. Every year he had to fetch an award. And he had to make sure no other actor could rise to his level.

For this, he nursed negative feelings like anger, bitterness and jealousy due to competitive instincts imposed upon him by co-actors, media, sycophants and fans. On the top of this, with age catching up, and the mirror repeatedly telling him the truth, and threat from the younger actors joining the race, feelings of great insecurity engulfed him. Hence, even at the peak of success, he was distressed by fear of failure.

The only way to cover up this fear was by projecting a larger-than-life persona. He projected himself as invincible, unconquerable. In the bargain, he became a compulsive attention seeker. As a result, at functions, events, parties or any other public gathering, if someone else besides him got any attention, he would get highly disturbed and end up deliberately doing something which diverts everyone's attention to him, like abusing or getting into a brawl. "I should not go unnoticed," was the only thing playing on his mind. And his drive to project himself as one of his kind made him too personalized. *My* perfume. *My* shoes. *My* shirt. To the extent, if he walked into a party where someone else was wearing the same watch as his, his mind would go for a toss.

Simultaneously, after achieving all the material comforts possible, he stopped getting anymore highs in life. And in order to stimulate himself, he got into weird things like promiscuous kinky sex, violence like driving recklessly and knocking down innocent pedestrians, and getting hooked on to drugs like cocaine.

Such behaviour translated itself into various kinds of physical and mental disorders, leaving his well-wishers extremely worried about his health. But he was on a maniacal trip where no one could control him. Not even his near and dear ones.

Amidst this chaotic life, there were phases when he desperately wanted to be left alone, but could not make it possible as the entire world was always waiting to catch him. Then he wondered if all the millions who claimed to be his die-hard fans really care about him. No. They only wanted to see him as an entertainer. No one was really bothered about what he was, what he felt, or what he desired as a human being.

But then, where were the people who really loved him as a human being? He realized he had driven them all away with his egomaniacal attitude. His personal life was a series of disastrous and painful relationships. His girlfriends, his wife, his children, parents and genuine friends could not cope with his wayward lifestyle and egocentric behaviour, and left or were asked to leave.

With so many people around, he felt so lonely, not being able to trust anyone who tried to come close to him, suspecting – usually correctly – him or her to be using him for some ulterior motive.

Unfortunately, even if someone was genuine, his distrusting eyes could not see the genuineness.

Today, at the peak of stardom, hailed to be as the biggest superstar, somewhere deep inside, Ronit yearns to be the common man, the simple unassuming middle-class boy he once was. But he is shattered to realize that come what may he will never again get a chance to be a common man.

As he concludes his address to his fans, he sombrely says, "I have given so many years of my life for your happiness. Now I want to find my own true happiness. My own peace of mind. For which I have to go. Let me go. Don't ever try to find me. That's the best token of love you can give me. Bye. Love you all."

As the screens go blank, the audience is highly moved, shaken up, speechless.

Meanwhile, sitting in the car parked in the dark deserted valley, Ronit has consumed enormous amounts of cocaine. Yet, he does not find peace. He sees flashes of many people, many places, many experiences that hammer at his mind like a machine gun.

He is menacingly bombarded by countless images, thoughts and sounds, making him highly agitated, suffocated and choked. Gasping for breath, he comes out of the car and violently pushes the car down the cliff.

Fighting extreme suffocation, he takes off his clothes and throws them away. Still, the bombardment of the thoughts, images and sounds only grows. He bangs his head on the rocks and his head starts bleeding profusely. But the onslaught does not stop. Blocking his ears with both his hands, shutting his eyes, he screams at the top of his voice. And as if to escape from his own self, he starts running crazily, without any sense of direction. Until he runs into the deep forests and gets lost in darkness.

That night, when Mikhil's mother opens the door to Mikhil, she is completely taken aback to see Mikhil totally overwhelmed. She lovingly asks him what made him so forlorn.

But Mikhil does not utter a word. He goes to his parents room and wakes up his father. Looking at Mikhil so distraught, his father is concerned too. In a solemn voice, Mikhil says, "Dad, I want to sit in our optician store from tomorrow."

Mikhil's parents are overjoyed by his decision.

THE END

CHAPTER SEVEN

FRIENDS FOREVER

When one's most fulfilling relationship comes in the form of friendship.

Amber Khurana, a hotshot ad film director from Mumbai, found everything and everyone in his life, including himself, terribly fake. He knew very well that all the social bees who exchanged 'sweetie', 'honey', 'darling', 'bro' by the dozen were doing so only out of some ulterior motive. Even his marriage of convenience with ex-supermodel Myra reeked of artificiality. Both of them had come to terms that their relationship was nothing more than a status-symbol.

Somewhere deep inside him, Amber missed a genuine relationship in his life. Because of this, he often recalls Meenakshi, his best friend in school fifteen years back, with whom he had lost touch after school. Though he tried often, he could not trace her in any social networking site.

Amber knew she was a very private person even in school and thus did not have much hopes of re-connecting with her ever again. Until one day, while browsing through TV channels, he spots Meenakshi on BBC in a talk show, representing her company Prime Madison based in San Francisco. Amber promptly uses his contacts abroad and manages to get her phone number.

Meenakshi, now an architect in San Francisco, is having a hard life. On the professional front, she has to struggle against subtle racial discrimination in the company she works in and on the personal front, she is subjected to constant bitterness and humiliation by her egocentric husband, Vinod. The latter was having an adverse effect on her five-year-old son, Rahul, as well. Yet, this does not shake her belief in the institution of marriage. And in order to make her marriage work, she regularly visits a marriage counsellor.

Given the volatility in her marriage, the counsellor suggests her to take a long break, which might give her husband time to analyse his behaviour, and also advises her to keep her son away from such an unpleasant environment.

As Meenakshi is jostling with such pressures, one day, she gets a surprise of her life. A phone call from her best friend from school, Amber!

In an instant, their spirits liven up. Just like in school, they start cracking up, pulling each other's leg, laughing like they had never laughed. From that day, life was no more so difficult for both of them, for they knew that every weekend they would talk on phone and pour out all their good and bad experiences to one another, taking off on everyone and never fail to laugh their guts out.

But one day turns out to be especially tough for Meenakshi, and she gives an unexpected call to Amber, the moment she hears his voice, she starts crying profusely. Amber tries to provide her solace, yet feels helpless as there is nothing he can do to sort out her troubles.

Meenakshi expresses, "I could never be happy after school. Just for once, I want to live my school days again."

Immediately, Amber cracks a plan. Meenakshi will come to Bangalore and drop her son to her mother. Then they shall meet in Delhi and stay with their school friend Debjyoti. After Delhi, they shall go to Goa to stay with their other school friend Anagha. At the end of trip, they will together come back to Bangalore and wish each other goodbye. Meenakshi is fine with the plan, but Amber lays down a condition, "When you come here, leave all your wounds behind. I want to meet the same Meenakshi I knew in school."

Henceforth, as Amber prepares for his trip, he recalls the moments when Meenakshi used to shell out money from her pocket money to give to Amber, so that he could go for movies with his boys group. Meenakshi, meanwhile, recalls how Amber used to pick up a brawl with just about anyone who spoke demeaning about Meenakshi.

Finally, as Amber waits for Meenakshi in Delhi Airport, he remembers the moment he confessed his love to Meenakshi and how shocked she was. She had said, "You know how strict my father is. I cannot even think of all this. All I am supposed to do is love the man my father will get me married to." At that moment, finding Meenakshi highly embarrassed, Amber had broken into a hearty laughter, telling Meenakshi he was only playing a prank on her. Even today, after fifteen years, as Amber's eyes get moist recalling that moment, his sight falls upon Meenakshi walking through the lobby towards him.

The moment they meet, like ever before, they are a house on fire! On their way to Debjyoti's house, as in school, in order to make the cab driver nervous, they act out a huge fight, leaving the cab driver completely flustered. But when they reach the locality in which Debjyoti stays, they are quite taken aback. This is not the kind of place they expected Debjyoti to stay in. It's a run-down unauthorized colony in Khan Market in Delhi.

Debjyoti, though was the most brilliant guy in studies, bursting with business ideas, could not do well in life. Married with two kids, he made a meagre living out of giving tuitions. Amber and Meenakshi, however, figure out the root problem. Though extremely talented, Debjyoti did not know how to market himself or project his innovative product (energizer herbal tablets) in the most lucrative way to prospective investors. Hence, a highly charged up mission breaks open to make Debjyoti street-smart and a marketing whiz.

While Meenakshi trains him in marketing techniques, Amber brushes him up in manipulation tricks, which he calls 'jugaadbaazi'. Initially, in meetings, Debjyoti ends up making goof ups after goof ups. But eventually, with Amber and Meenakshi hauling him up, he starts improving. What's more, Meenakshi prepares a highly professional power–point presentation for him. And Amber creates an elaborate advertising campaign, even though he has a harrowing time shooting a mock ad film with Debjyoti and Meenakshi as models. Eventually, finally, eureka!

Debjyoti gets an investor for his business.

All this while, Amber continues to fulfil his promise to Meenakshi of re-living school days. As they hold singing sessions while Debjyoti plays guitar, imitate their teachers and hog on mango-meals, Amber expresses to Meenakshi how trapped he felt being in an environment where everyone including him is so fake.

As in school, Meenakshi always attempted to find a solution for Amber, even now, Meenakshi says, "You are in a fake environment, but you can be genuine in your creative work. Why don't you make a feature film with utmost honesty, in which you can pour out all your genuine thoughts and purest feelings."

Motivated by Meenakshi, that whole night, Amber enthusiastically writes a storyline for a movie with the title 'SAAHIL'. And the next day, when he reads it out aloud to Meenakshi, Debjyoti and family, he is responded with a hearty applause. Amber is on cloud nine that he got a way to be genuine once again.

Later, as Debjyoti and Amber go out to a pub as their last night together on this trip, over drinks Debjyoti expresses how everybody in the class felt that he and Meenakshi were made for each other. He asserts that it was still not too late. Both are having a dissatisfying marriage. They needed to be happy. And their happiness lies in each other.

As Debjyoti cajoles Amber to think on these lines, Amber says, "Even if I think so, I know that Meenakshi will never think on these lines."

Debjyoti further asserts, "Give her so much happiness in this trip that she is left with no option but to start thinking on these lines."

Consequently, as Amber and Meenakshi prepare to go to Goa, Debjyoti's words keep replaying in Amber's mind. Finally, they reach Anagha's house in Goa – a huge, opulent bungalow.

Anagha had all the comforts and pleasures in the world, or so it seemed, until, Amber and Meenakshi discover that Anagha was languishing in a loveless marriage. Though Anagha was a die-hard romantic, her husband Mayur was the most unromantic man and most of the times away on business trips.

Anagha confides, "I am anticipating that this time when he returns from his business trip, he might declare that he wants a separation."

Amber and Meenakshi have all the sympathies for Anagha until they realize the core problem that Anagha was only romantic and there was nothing more to her. She just did not know about anything in the world except films and TV serials. As a result, in spite of acting very exciting, she came across as utterly boring.

Amber and Meenakshi decide to wake her up, shake her up. All through their stay, they completely ban Films and TV and transform Anagha into a woman of substance for which she needed grilling training sessions. And since 'learning' was a huge phobia for Anagha, she goes through a harrowing time having to learn so many things in so less time.

Big fear –learning to use ATM. Bigger fear - learning to drive. Biggest fear – learning to use a computer. Much against her will, under strict dictatorship of her friends, she has to learn all of it.

Big bore – reading books on general knowledge. Bigger bore – listening to lectures on spiritualism. Biggest bore - watching news. She has to do it all as Amber and Meenakshi refuse to talk to her about anything except 'knowledge'.

By the time Mayur returns home from his business trip, he finds a new woman as his wife. Anagha's entire personality has enhanced by leaps and bounds. So overwhelming, that seeing her, now her husband becomes a romantic.

All this while, when Anagha was put through various exercises, Amber and Meenakshi continue with their own agenda of reliving school days. They create ruckus in a cinema hall by loudly revealing the story of the film. They dance to old numbers in 'Shammi Kapoor' style. They make people 'bakra' on the street. But this time, the way Amber looks at Meenakshi is different – as if he was looking for the moment where Meenakshi starts looking at him as more than just a friend. And he feels the time has arrived when Meenakshi confides in him how miserable she was in her marriage and she was living under constant stress.

Amber responds, "I remember that you use to attend classical dance Bharat Natyam classes. And you use to say that dancing was a heavenly experience for you. Why don't you resume dancing? That will surely take away all your stress."

Next day, Amber takes Meenakshi to a park. Much to her surprise, Amber plays classical music on his laptop and persuades Meenakshi to dance. As Meenakshi starts dancing, her joy knows no bounds and she dances her way to complete ecstasy. Out of sheer delight, Meenakshi runs to Amber and hugs him tightly and thanks him. Amber feels confident that she had come to a stage where she would think of him in a special way.

In the evening, as their last night in Goa, Amber and Meenakshi come with Anagha and Mayur to a pub with a dance floor. As everybody gets comfortable, Amber sends a request to the DJ and the DJ plays the song 'How Deep is Your Love' which was Meenakshi's favourite song.

Meenakshi is overwhelmed to hear the song. Seeing her so elated, Amber walks up to her and offers her a dance. Though Meenakshi is hesitant, everybody coaxes her and she has to give in. As Amber and Meenakshi dance on this soft romantic number, Amber looks continuously into Meenakshi's eyes lovingly which makes her feel awkward. Then, as Amber physically tries to get closer and intimate with her, Meenakshi feels more and more awkward. Eventually, she completely withdraws and leaves the pub. And Amber feels dejected.

As a flustered Meenakshi stands alone at the beach, Amber appears looking for her. He spots her from a distance and walks up to her and stands next to her. In a sombre tone, he says, "So, can't we ever be together?"

Meenakshi firmly replies, "I have a child. For the sake of my child, I will have to work out things with his father. Come what may. If you would have had a child from your wife, you would have understood."

Meenakshi starts walking away until Amber calls out, "Meenakshi, you know we are made for each other."

Meenakshi turns back and replies, "We are still there for each other. As friends. We need no labels, Amber. When a beautiful bond is difficult to exist in one form, make it exist in some other form." With this, Meenakshi walks away leaving Amber alone and crestfallen.

All through their way to Bangalore, while Meenakshi tries her best to be cheerful, Amber remains upset. Finally, as the cab reaches Meenakshi's mother's house, Meenakshi asks Amber to come in for coffee but Amber does not respond. Seeing him so unrelenting, Meenakshi can't help saying, "Amber, by behaving like this, you are destroying our friendship. Don't do this. This is the most precious thing I have."

Before she can say anything further, her son Rahul comes running from inside and Meenakshi gets engaged with him. Rahul exclaims, "Papa said on phone he will buy a new play station when I go back."

Amber notices how many plans Meenakshi's son had made with his father. Before he leaves, Meenakshi asks, "Will you come to see me off at the airport tomorrow?"

"I don't know," Amber curtly replies and leaves in the cab.

Amber then checks into a hotel. As he settles in his room, he is listless, forlorn. Just as he is lost in melancholy, he receives a phone call from his wife Myra. She breaks in the good news, "Sweetie, guess what? I am pregnant. You are going to be a father."

Suddenly, the world lightens up for Amber. In sheer joy, he jumps and breaks into a rigorous jig, screaming euphorically, repeatedly, "I am going to be a father!"

Finally, when he is completely exhausted, he crashes on the bed, there is great sense of fulfilment and peace on his face. He recalls Meenakshi's words, "If you would have had a child from your wife, you would have understood."

Next evening, we see Amber moving in a cab pleasantly recalling images of all the moments he shared with Meenakshi.

As Meenakshi reaches the airport with Rahul, she finds that Amber is already present there waiting for her. As Rahul goes to buy chocolates, Meenakshi tells Amber, "I knew you would come."

Amber cheerfully replies, "I had to come. We can't get rid of each other. You know why? Because we are soul-mates. We have to meet each other in every lifetime. So what if not in this lifetime? We will get married in some other lifetime."

Meenakshi smiles and gives Amber a gift. In return, Amber too gives her a gift. Then, Meenakshi with Rahul say 'bye' to Amber and walk in to the lobby.

As Meenakshi is walking towards the check in counter, Amber can see her going. As Meenakshi walks, images of all the moments she shared with Amber cross her mind. And then, completely overwhelmed, she suddenly stops. She turns back and looks at Amber.

Amber too keeps looking at her. Slowly, Meenakshi starts walking towards him. Amber is overwhelmed to see her coming towards him. Finally, she comes and stands very close to him. There are volumes spoken through silence and their wet eyes. As if ice is going to be broken this very moment, suddenly, Rahul calls out to Meenakshi and her thought is broken. She, in a broken voice, tells Amber, "I'll keep calling you."

Amber, in a choked voice, replies, "You have to."

Meenakshi turns and walks into the airport.

When a beautiful bond is difficult to exist in one form, make it exist in some other form.

Later, as Amber moves in a cab, he unwraps the gift Meenakshi gave him. It is a clapper board for his film with the title 'SAAHIL'. Amber is ecstatic looking at it.

Meenakshi, on the other end, unwraps the gift Amber gave her. Looking at it her face brightens up. It is a pair of 'ghunghroos'.

Amber and Meenakshi go back to their usual life, yet they never miss talking to each other on phone every weekend.

In one phone call, Amber enthusiastically informs, "Guess what? My film is going on floors in July."

In another phone call, Meenakshi informs, "You know what? I have joined a weekly dance academy."

The phone calls continue. The friendship continues.

THE END